The Awful Aardvarks
SHOP FOR SCHOOL

by
Reeve Lindbergh

illustrated by
Tracey Campbell Pearson

VIKING

VIKING
Published by the Penguin Group
Penguin Putnam Books for Young Readers, 345 Hudson Street, New York, New York 10014, U.S.A.
Penguin Books Ltd, 27 Wrights Lane, London W8 5TZ, England
Penguin Books Australia Ltd, Ringwood, Victoria, Australia
Penguin Books Canada Ltd, 10 Alcorn Avenue, Toronto, Ontario, Canada M4V 3B2
Penguin Books (N.Z.) Ltd, 182-190 Wairau Road, Auckland 10, New Zealand

Penguin Books Ltd, Registered Offices: Harmondsworth, Middlesex, England

First published in 2000 by Viking, a division of Penguin Putnam Books for Young Readers.

1 3 5 7 9 10 8 6 4 2

Text copyright © Reeve Lindbergh, 2000
Illustrations copyright © Tracey Campbell Pearson, 2000
All rights reserved

LIBRARY OF CONGRESS CATALOGING-IN-PUBLICATION DATA
Lindbergh, Reeve.
The awful Aardvarks shop for school / by Reeve Lindbergh; illustrated by Tracey Campbell Pearson.
p.   cm.
Summary: Aardvarks invade the Shop-All-Day Mall and turn it upside down with their wild back-to-school shopping spree.
ISBN 0-670-88763-3 (hc)
[1. Shopping malls—Fiction. 2. Aardvark—Fiction. 3. Stories in rhyme.] I. Pearson, Tracey Campbell, ill. II. Title.
PZ8.3.L6148 Ax 2000 [E]—dc21 99-059259

Printed in Hong Kong
Set in Sabon

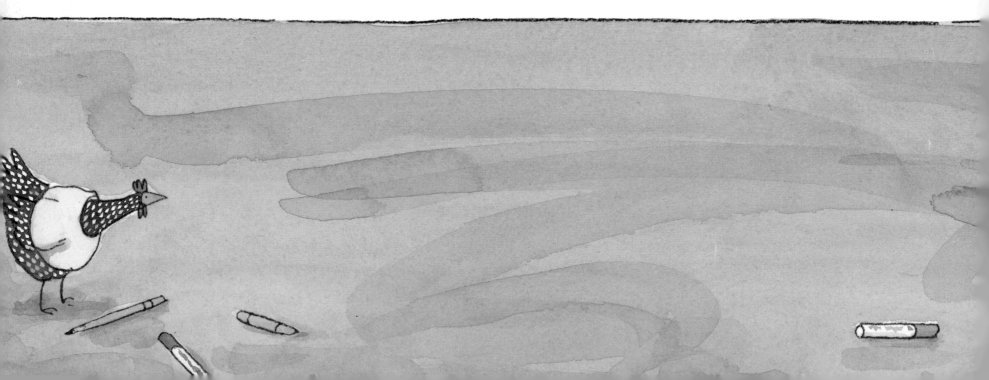

For Ella Jane, who is awfully awesome
—R. L.

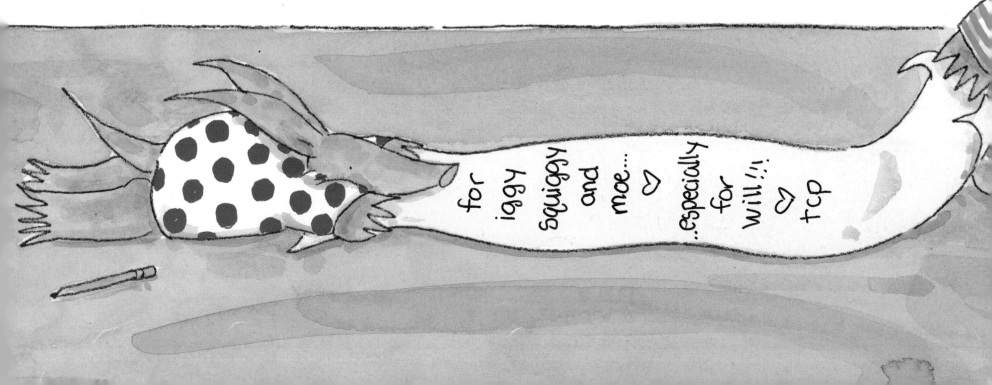

SHOPPING LIST

sneakers
(for sports)
new jackets

notebooks
pencils
crayons
glue
fat markers
skinny too!
markers
lunch box
(with thermos)
backpacks
Haircuts

Without any warning, one morning in fall,
the Aardvarks invaded the Shop-All-Day Mall.

Their back-to-school list read, "Get sneakers for sports,"
but instead they tried sunglasses, T-shirts, and shorts . . .

SHOP ING LIST

sneakers
(for sports)
new jackets

notebooks
pencils
crayons
glue
fat markers
skinny too!
markers
lunch box
(with thermos)
backpacks

Haircuts!

. . . and face masks, and helmets, and pads for their knees.
Then they raced off on Rollerblades, skateboards, and skis.

SHOPPING LIST

sneakers (for sports)
new jackets
notebooks
pencils
crayons
glue
fat markers
skinny too!
markers
lunch box
(with thermos)
backpacks
Haircuts!

"New jackets," the list read; they found some with feathers.
They also found jewelry, and laces, and leathers.

SHOPPING LIST

scissors
(fat markers)
new jackets

notebooks
pencils
crayons
glue
fat markers
skinny too!
markers
lunch box
(with thermos)
backpacks

Haircuts!

"Buy notebooks, and pencils, and crayons, and glue.
Buy markers—get fat ones, and skinny ones, too."

"A lunch box with thermos," the list read, but where?
A sign pointed: toy store. The Aardvarks tried there.

TINA'S
TIMELESS
TOYS
→

They tried all the trucks and they tried all the trains.
They tried Alien games till they frazzled their brains.

There wasn't a lunch box—they had to move on.
(The man in the store was SO happy they'd gone.)

"Backpacks" were next, and they saw quite a few,
But they also saw SWEETS (and they gobbled them, too).

SHOPPING LIST

sneakers
(for sports)
new jackets

notebooks
pencils
crayons
glue

~~markers~~
~~box~~
~~markers~~
~~box~~
(with thermos)
backpacks
~~~~cuts!

Their faces were sticky, their hands were a mess.
The shopkeepers started to show signs of stress.

Then they spotted the bookstore that's called Bears and Bubbles, and that's where the Aardvarks began to have troubles.

All the shoppers stopped shopping and gave them weird looks.
The Aardvarks were stuck—they were stuck to the books!

They panicked and ran. They ran faster and faster, flew into the Food Court—was THAT a disaster!

SHOPPING LIST

sneakers
(for sports)
new jacket
notebook
pencils
crayons
glue
fat markers
skinny too!
marker
lunchbox
(with thermos)
backpacks
Haircuts!

They slipped in the salad bar. Oh, how distressing!
They were dripping with lettuce and drenched in French dressing.

They hopped in the bagel bin, hoping to hide,
but the Bagel Boy caught them and dragged them outside.

"Stop!" yelled the Bagel Boy. "Promise you will!
Take everything back and clean up every spill!"

SHOPPING LIST

~~sneakers~~
~~(for sports)~~
~~new jackets~~

~~notebooks~~
~~pencils~~
~~crayons~~
~~glue~~
~~fat markers~~
~~skinny too!~~
~~markers~~
~~lunchbox~~
~~(with thermos)~~
~~backpacks~~

Nobody spoke (maybe nobody dared).
The Aardvarks looked worried, and sorry, and scared.

SHOPPING LIST

sneakers
(for sports)
new jackets

notebooks
pencils
crayons

But then they cleaned up and returned all the stuff,
Till the shopkeepers said, "That's okay! That's enough!"

SHOPPING LIST

sneakers
(for sports-)
new jackets
notebooks
pencils
crayons
glue
felt markers
(any too)
mark
lunch
(with
backpac
haircuts!

Their faces still sticky, their hands still a mess,
the list read, "get haircuts." The Aardvarks said, "YES!"

They got shampooed and manicured, permed and perfumed,
and when they were finished away they all zoomed.

SHOPPING LIST

~~sneakers~~
~~(for sports)~~
~~new jackets~~

~~notebooks~~
~~pencils~~
~~crayons~~
~~glue~~
~~fat markers~~
~~skinny too!~~
~~markers~~
~~lunchbox~~
~~(with thermos)~~
~~backpacks~~

~~Haircuts!~~

As the Aardvarks danced happily out of the mall,
"Good-bye," they all shouted, "we'll see you next fall!"